Winifred and Maggie

Their Music Adventure

Jeannene Pettett Hall

Illustrated by Joshua Allen

AuthorHouse™
1663 Liberty Drive
Bloomington, IN 47403
www.authorhouse.com
Phone: 1 (800) 839-8640

Published by AuthorHouse 06/27/2016

ISBN: 978-1-5246-0929-0 (sc)
978-1-5246-0931-3 (hc)
978-1-5246-0930-6 (e)

Library of Congress Control Number: 2016908082

Print information available on the last page.

Any people depicted in stock imagery provided by Thinkstock are models,
and such images are being used for illustrative purposes only.
Certain stock imagery © Thinkstock.

This book is printed on acid-free paper.

authorHOUSE®

For Emma, I love you dearly and will be there for you every step of the way.

The sun is shining through the window

Wake up sleeping Winifred.

Wake up sleeping Maggie.

Today is music class, so we must start our day.

Brush, brush, brush our teeth.

Comb, comb, comb our hair.

Wash, wash, wash our face.

Time to pick our clothes to wear!

Mommy is in the kitchen making breakfast.

It's Winifred's favorite breakfast,--scrambled eggs with cheese.

Maggie eats her dog food in her own special bowl.

When everyone is finished, it is off to class we go.

We are riding in the car, all buckled up.

Red light, red light! We must stop.

Green light, green light! We can go.

Music class is just around the corner.

Look! There's our music class.

Maggie runs in the door.

Winifred starts to feel shy.

Maybe she will go back to the car.

"It's time for music class, Winifred," her friends say.

"We know you feel shy, so let's all go in together," they say.

All the dogs are going through the door.

Winifred sings to the music.

She dances with her friends.

She plays all the different instruments.

But soon class will end.

Music class is almost over.

They sing their good-bye song.

Winifred hugs all her friends.

She tells Maggie to come along.

Winifred tells her Mommy all about her class.

Winifred is happy she decided to go.

"Let's go get a snack," Mommy says.

Winifred loves her Mommy and Maggie so.

Thanks to Robyn Bauer, Director of Bright Beginnings Music Together, and teachers Ms. Kendra and Ms. Adele, for providing a wonderful music experience for children. The musical environment and dedication to your students is unsurpassed. Thank you for bringing out the musical passion in my daughter.

Below are some photos that I would like to share of the Music Together class and some photos of our sweet Maggie.

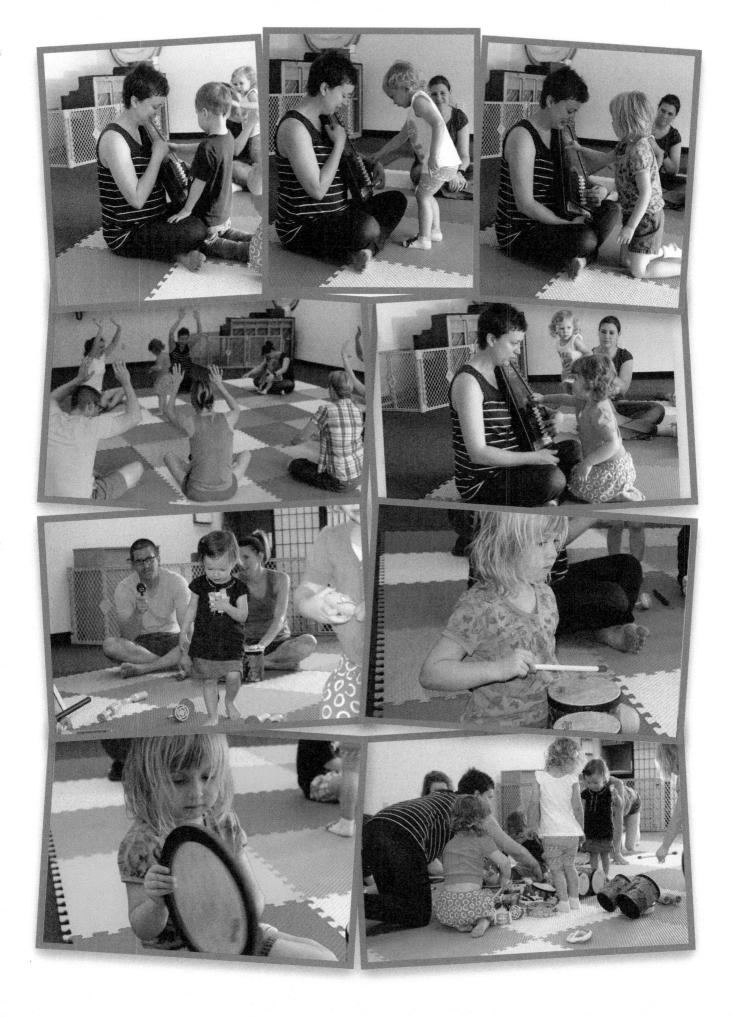

CPSIA information can be obtained at www.ICGtesting.com
Printed in the USA
BVOW05s2115050816

458135BV00002B/3/P

9 781524 609290